W9-AWE-369

LARRY POTTER™

and His Best Friend Lilly™

written and illustrated by

N.K. STOUFFER

Thurman House
Owings Mills, MD

Larry Potter is a friend of Lilly's

He has beautiful, big brown eyes,

But Larry is now very sad,

And Lilly wonders why.

Lilly tries her very best,

But Larry just won't join the rest.

She brings him flowers....

wouldn't you?

And a box of candy

...maybe two!

She dances, and she sings awhile...

But Larry doesn't even smile!

Lilly must do something...

She knocks on every
neighborhood door,

And gathers all of Larry's
best friends,

She needs their help
and even more...

They got together in the park,

To come up with a plan...

They want their good friend,
Larry,

To smile and laugh again.

They came up with an answer,

A party's just the thing;

And so they made arrangements

For what each one should bring.

Ice cream, balloons, and presents...

What fun this surprise will be,

But friends are just not ready...

For the surprise that they will see.

When one is getting glasses,

There's a challenge to be met,

Fears that life will really change

Can make you most upset.

But true friends really like you,

For simply who you are;

It doesn't matter what you wear,

Or whether you're a star.

And, when good friend Larry,

Walks in through that door,

He looks so very different...

Then he even looked before.

No, it surely isn't Larry's smile

That seems so out-of-place;

It's the brand new pair of glasses,

That they see on Larry's face.

Now his friends all really know

Why Larry Potter was so blue,

But the boys didn't mind the glasses,

And the girls thought they were cute,

And Larry can see more clearly now

Than he ever saw before;

He saw that they were *true* friends,

When he walked through that door.